W9-AAW-292

821.8
Lea   Lear, Edward, 1812-1888.
       An Edward Lear alphabet

DATE DUE

MY 10 '00			

BANNOCKBURN SCHOOL DIST. 106
2165 TELEGRAPH ROAD
DEERFIELD, ILLINOIS 60015

DEMCO

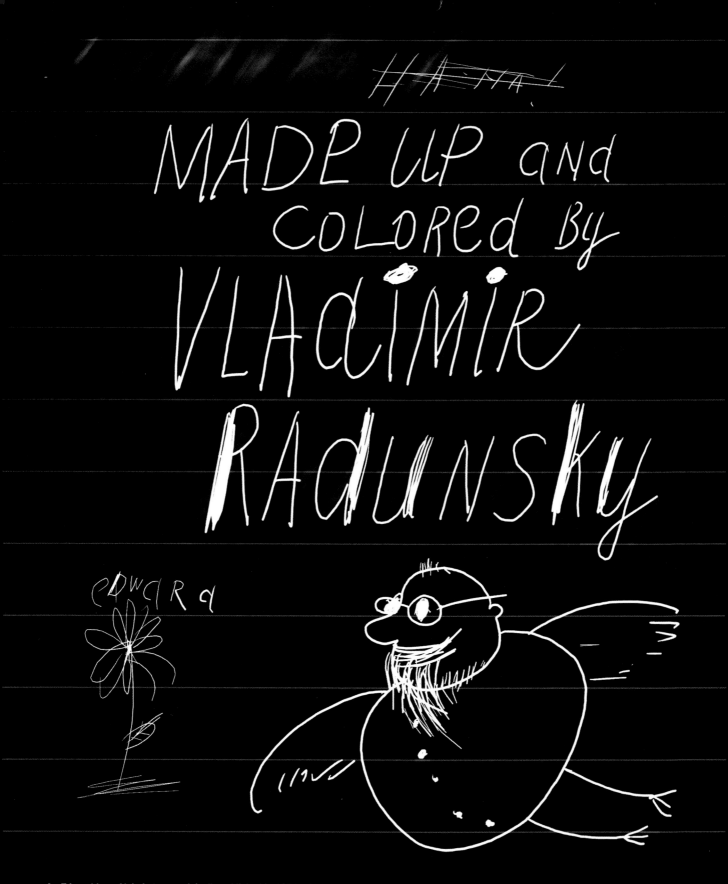

MADE UP and
COLORED BY
VLADIMIR
RADUNSKY

An Edward Lear Alphabet was originally published in 1871. An Edward Lear Alphabet. All new materials copyright © 1999 by HarperCollins

Publishers Inc. Illustrations copyright © 1999 Vladimir Radunsky. Printed in the USA. All rights reserved. Library of Congress catalog card

number: 98-27496. Visit our web site at http://www.harperchildrens.com. Designed by Vladimir Radunsky 1 2 3 4 5 6 7 8 9 10 ❖ First Edition

An Edward Lear

ALPHABET

BANNOCKBURN SCHOOL DIST. 106
2165 TELEGRAPH ROAD
DEERFIELD, ILLINOIS 60015

 HARPERCOLLINSPUBLISHERS

A was once an apple pie,
Pidy
Widy
Tidy
Pidy
Nice insidy
Apple pie.

B was once a little bear,
Beary
Wary
Hairy
Beary
Taky cary
Little bear.

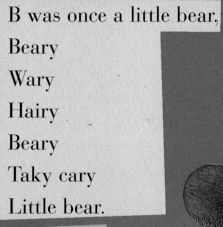

C

C was once a little cake,
Caky
Baky
Maky
Caky
Taky caky
Little cake.

D

D was once a little doll,
Dolly
Molly
Polly
Nolly
Nursy dolly
Little doll.

E

E was once a little eel,
Eely
Weely
Peely
Eely
Twirly tweely
Little eel.

F

F was once a little fish,
Fishy
Wishy
Squishy
Fishy
In a dishy
Little fish.

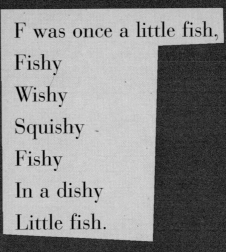

G was once a little goose,
Goosy
Moosy
Boosey
Goosey
Waddly woosy
Little goose.

G

H was once a little hen,
Henny
Chenny
Tenny
Henny
Eggsy any
Little hen.

I was once a bottle of ink,
Inky
Dinky
Thinky
Inky
Blacky minky
Bottle of ink.

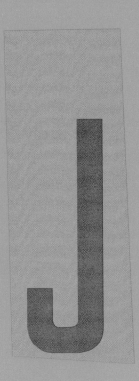

J was once a jar of jam,
Jammy
Mammy
Clammy
Jammy
Sweety swammy
Jar of jam.

K

K was once a little kite,
Kity
Whity
Flighty
Kity
Out of sighty
Little kite.

L

L was once a little lark,
Larky
Marky
Harky
Larky
In the parky
Little lark.

M was once a little mouse,
Mousey
Bousey
Sousy
Mousy
In the housy
Little mouse.

N was once a little needle,
Needly
Tweedly
Threedly
Needly
Wisky wheedly
Little needle.

O

O was once a little owl,
Owly
Prowly
Howly
Owly
Browny fowly
Little owl.

P was once a little pump,
Pumpy
Slumpy
Flumpy
Pumpy
Dumpy thumpy
Little pump.

Q was once a little quail,
Quaily
Faily
Daily
Quaily
Stumpy taily
Little quail.

Q

R was once a little rose,
Rosy
Posy
Nosy
Rosy
Blows-y grows-y
Little rose.

S

S was once a little shrimp,
Shrimpy
Nimpy
Flimpy
Shrimpy
Jumpy jimpy
Little shrimp.

T

T was once a little thrush,
Thrushy
Hushy
Bushy
Thrushy
Flitty flushy
Little thrush.

U

U was once a little urn,
Urny
Burny
Turny
Urny
Bubbly burny
Little urn.

V was once a little vine,
Viny
Winy
Twiny
Viny
Twisty twiny
Little vine.

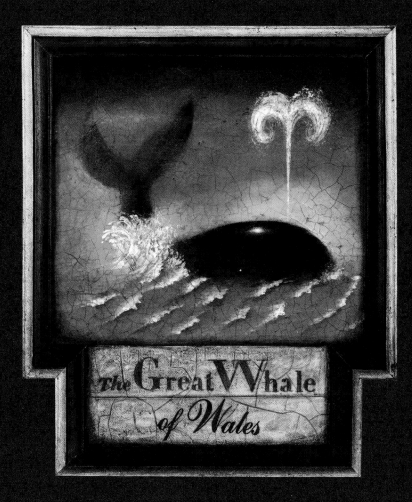

The Great Whale of Wales

W

W was once a whale,
Whaly
Scaly
Shaly
Whaly
Tumbly taily
Mighty whale.

X was once a great king Xerxes,
Xerxy
Perxy
Turxy
Xerxy
Linxy Lurxy
Great King Xerxes.

Y

Y was once a little Yew,
Yewdy
Fewdy
Crudy
Yewdy
Growdy grewdy
Little yew.

Z was once a piece of zinc,
Tinky
Winky
Blinky
Tinky
Tinkly minky
Piece of zinc.

BANNOCKBURN SCHOOL DIST. 106
2165 TELEGRAPH ROAD
DEERFIELD, ILLINOIS 60015

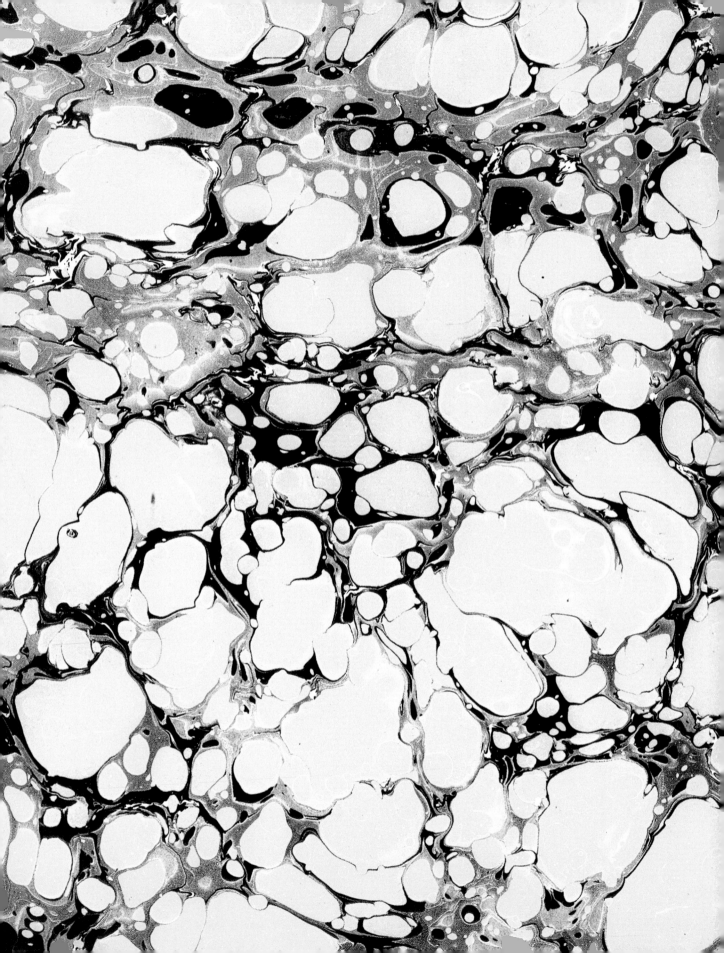